SEA PASSAGES

Published by Seilachan Fort

ISBN: 978-0-9933887-3-6

Contents

Foreword

I feel privileged to introduce this wee book of ferry stories harvested from the creative talents of writers who have dropped anchor in and around the harbour town of Oban in the West Highlands of Scotland.

Each writer has tied up alongside the safe berth of Argyll College at some time or other and it was there that I had the pleasure of listening to and reading their work. The idea for a themed short story anthology first surfaced a good few years ago and like a fine Highland malt, I hope you'll agree it has been worth the wait.

I would particularly like to thank Roxanne and also Denise and her team, who made this project happen; my fellow writers for allowing me the honour of being part of this barnacle-encrusted bonanza of stories and lastly, as always, to the people of the West Coast of Scotland, without whom we would have no stories to tell.

Alex Breck

Dead In The Water
by Alex Breck

The stranger stood tall at the head of the boat, the silhouette of his upturned face sharp like a knife against the bloodless sky as yet another angry flash of lightning seared across the Minch.

"At least the weather's the bloody same!"

He bowed his head in mock respect and turned towards the other 'grief-stricken' passengers who were following the old highland tradition of making the best of a sad occasion by making a right good party of it. The rain joined in with a demonic dance across the decks and so he pulled the brim of his hat lower over his face and edged closer, remaining more or less invisible despite his height. Over the years he'd learnt a lot about people just by listening. He'd become extremely adept at shameless eavesdropping and had no qualms whatsoever about his outrageous invasions of people's privacy as he would absorb the valuable lessons from the slings and arrows of their lives. Even now, above the roaring of the wind and the waves, he could just make out various conversations about the unfortunate bloke who was recently deceased; some good, some bad, all exaggerated of course and blacker than the truth.

"Aye, ah heard he'd faither'd mair than jist the wan bairn afore he flew the coop!"

"No, but, they say he's gied the island a guid few boab back like. Mair than 'abody from 'oor faimly has ever done, 'ken what ah'm saying?"

"Ah heard that an' all but. The devil's wages though, eh?"

"I know! D'ye think it's right? That he really was murder't?"

The tall stranger turned away and gazed out over the choppy sea towards the dark mass of the approaching island. He'd not heard the authentic Scots' voice much over the last couple of decades but it hadn't lost that innate capacity for twisting the knife, not just for kicking a guy when he was down but driving a fucking bus over him as well.

There was no denying he'd done well for himself since he'd left. His tailored black suit probably cost as much as most of the battered old cars down below deck. He was able to take a black cab all the way from Glasgow Airport and have it sitting on the pier for the next few days on stand-by. Just in case. He smiled grimly to himself. *But not exactly the return of the Prodigal is it?* In fact, he was probably the last person most passengers on this boat would want to see. He'd done some evil and monstrous things since his last voyage on this ferry, far worse than the dark deed that had him driven from these islands long ago. But he wanted to put all of that behind him now and after this one last terrible thing, he hoped to bury his past and finally be himself. He knew deep down in his desolate heart that, even for him, this last thing might prove to be a step too far, a journey into an everlasting hell.

The icy wind whipped at his wet coat and the man moved across the rolling deck with casual purpose towards the huddled passengers sheltering by the twin funnels belching out their stale warm air. He saw some he thought he recognised, but they all seemed to have *filled out*, their faces aged and bloated, rusted and worn out like this tired old ferry. Unbidden images surfaced from the depths and he remembered light and airy crossings filled with the endless sunshine and optimism of his youth. Too soon, the lightning flashed and in that brief moment his eyes met those of another man, their faces illuminated in the gloom. He ducked and turned but too late! He saw the spark of recognition quickly moving from confusion to fear as the murky night encroached once again.

A young girl staggered against the railings as the ferry lurched downwards into a trough of ink black swirling water. To him she looked fragile, just like a new-born calf, her long skinny legs struggling to keep the rest of her body upright as the ferry rolled with the waves. Glancing directly up at him, he was struck by her huge eyes, dark with smudged mascara adding to their vulnerable intensity. The girl smiled politely. He nodded and thought for the hundredth time that day about his own daughter Caitlin, who'd be about the same age.

The daughter he would see for the first time the very next day.

He'd seen pictures of course. His old mum had always been very good at slipping the odd photo away from Caitlin's mother Morag, whom she'd only barely tolerated. She'd been heartbroken at how easily history could be re-written when Morag, just a child herself, had hastily married another so soon after her seventeen-year-old sweetheart had abandoned her at the mainland ferry terminal and fled to the big city, so the story went. She hadn't known that he'd been beaten unconscious and thrown onto the early morning London train, his bloodied ears ringing with the promise of violence to his entire family if he ever returned. No-one had known she was already carrying his child.

But now he was back. And a completely different proposition from the penniless young boy who'd last traversed this bleak sea.

He'd eventually washed up in a primordial swamp outside Newcastle; in 'hard man country' where he'd learned to wield a baseball bat instead of a shinty stick. He fought his way into 'security work' at the steelworks and then the docks. He didn't say much but listened well and learnt a lot. By good fortune he came across as a lot more scary than he actually was and soon he made the harsh and alien world he found himself inhabiting into his own fiefdom. He branched out into property, taking advantage of council 'right-to-buy' schemes and buying up rows of houses from little old ladies who were more than happy to pay him £20 less in weekly rent than they'd been paying the council in return for signing some paperwork for him. When, unavoidably, they departed hence, the houses were his and at the last count he'd become the owner of over 100 properties worth several million. All of which he'd just sold.

So here he was. Not quite alone, however. His demons both real and imagined were also lurking in the hidden depths of the ferry. Most of them would be in the bar down below, their Sassenach constitutions too soft to endure the bracing Scottish hospitality up here in the open. Besides, he knew how their savage minds worked. They'd be partying around the coffin, a drunken guard of dishonour. If they could get away with it they'd have the lid off. Just to be sure. They would have sore heads in the morning, he knew from experience and he wondered who'd be carrying the coffin up the long, steep drag of the Bealach to the old cemetery. *Not me, that's for sure.*

There had been a pact made with the Devil he knew that. The stakes were high and he had no delusions that his plans would be totally successful. Lightning cracked across the bow and only one figure stood tall against the powerful array of elemental forces against him. In the brief coruscating white light, a trickle of jet black fluid could be seen under his nose. *A gift from my gene pool*, he muttered darkly as he swiftly dabbed at his face. Another demon come to haunt him from the past.

His grandfather had made this same ferry trip many years previous. Attempting to escape from the harrowing triple whammy of the pernicious disease, grinding poverty and criminal depravity of East End Glasgow, he'd worked himself into an early grave to forge a new life on the island. His son had gone on to embrace the highland traditions of croft, creel and *craic* and had been devastated to all but lose his only son at seventeen. All of this had to be part of the bargain, to right the wrongs of the past and to set the future on a brighter course.

The cantankerous ferry creaked and groaned as if being wrenched apart by the stormy sea and as he looked up towards the glass of the wheelhouse he swore he could see a diabolical red gleam from within. *Aye*, he thought, *it's Auld Nick steering this boat tonight*.

Tomorrow there would be a funeral, an ending but also a beginning. He would meet his daughter and invite her to come away with him to a sunnier land where anything was possible, even for him. But although they had been in touch via the internet, a persistent worry plagued him, worse than a sheepdog nipping at your ankles. He still couldn't be sure how it would go with Caitlin when they actually met in person. He shivered and then swallowed and tasted the salt air on his lips. Doubt was beginning to insinuate its way into his bones like the cold black rain.

Tomorrow would be also his last ever day of work, a job that would make a stamp on history and forever silence his demons. He knew he'd the perfect alibi for an audacious crime of the like never seen since the days of the Great Train Robbery.

In a fiendish reply, the old ferry dropped her bow and plummeted to the depths, leaving the grim-faced passengers stumbling and grappling for hand-holds before the inevitable thunderous crashing as the boat wrought herself free and pointed two grimy fingers at the starless sky.

All but one.

The tall stranger stood alone, strong as the elements raging against him. As they huddled together like frightened children, some of the others stared aghast at his foolish behaviour, possibly thinking him demented, perhaps by grief.

But he just looked back at them all and smiled.

He knew where he was going. There was just one other niggling worry on his mind. Just what was the proper etiquette for attending your own funeral?

Sale Day
by Roxanne MacColl

A ferry story? Aye, I can tell you a ferry story. A story from when I first came here, from when I thought everything was quaint and idyllic. From when I could still be surprised by how much it rained, from when I didn't keep a change of clothes and a tenner in the car for when the ferry didn't run. From when I didn't say 'aye'.

We made it in good time for the ferry that day, and the tourists sitting in the restaurant at the top of the pier came out to see the arrival of our sheep trailers, full of tups bought at the sale, pulled by cars full of families.

They watched as we paraded in our town clothes: bright colours, ribbons and silks and children and laughter in the air; snatches of song and cajoling and a bottle passed back and forth. The animals snorted and coughed, their breath savage, but we were happy with the day's trade and shushed them like we did the wee ones, trying to keep everyone, and the shopping, out of the water.

When they were pulled out of the trailers the sheep spun like dervishes, hooves tip-tipping on the concrete. With shouts we fell back then quickly herded them close, but they were blinded by the sudden light and frightened by the smell of the sea, and not easily calmed. The men walked the beasts down to the boat, each man caging one between his knees, holding them by horns or coat. Some had fierce curling horns; some long necks: snake like. Some of the sheep had heads like anvils and tiny, rolling eyes.

We women followed, trailing bags and children's coats. The sky was a clear September blue and the air crisp. The breeze off the water lifted our voices over the sea and the gulls cried in response. The hills of Morven stood proud and close behind the island, where we could see people, lorries and trailers already gathering on the slip to help take us home.

One by one, the sheep were wrestled onto the ferry, and they stood and heaved and moaned against the legs of the people who blocked their escape.

The skipper was jovial, calling to the men to "Hold! Hold! Watch it now! Aye the wee bugger's no match for you!" and to the children to "settle, settle, do you want a shot at the wheel?" and to the woman only a gentlemanly nod and "good day for it, aye?" as we paid our fares. He'd done this before.

He didn't notice the foetid, thick smell of steaming wool mingling with the sweet scent of whisky and the milky smell of sleepy babies. It seemed to stay the boat, tethering us to the shore, and we crossed the loch slowly.

As we rounded the beacon, the sea - at the pier clear enough to see the wee, quick fish and star fish on the sandy floor - became suddenly dark. The wind began to gust, breaking waves against the sides of the boat and moving us more determinedly through the water. The ferry turned towards the slip and the animals grew restless again, huffing and butting their heads against our knees and each other. We began to gather our things, counting bags and children, fastening jackets and putting up hoods, jerking around the boat to avoid the sea spray and odd angry horn.

The boat reached the slip with a rush, bags spilling apples and loaves that were crushed under boots and hooves as we struggled to contain the animals and keep our footing.

One by one, each animal was restrained and heads aimed for the doorway. The slip on this side was narrow, slick with weed, long in the low tide. Men and woman started down to lend a hand as we arranged to leave the boat. First at the door, first out: no parades in this rain. Ian had hold of a black faced tup, and I saw him lose his footing. As he tried to right himself, I watched as he lost his grip on the horns of the beast. A terror loosed: but the group on the slip held firm and it was caught, with only pride hurt.

Our tup in its box, we walked back to the slip to lend a last hand, lingering at the top to say our farewells and pass on last bits of news as the trail of people and animals passed us.

Then, as though the ground itself was shaking, the men still on the slip began to fall: shoving, shouting, others running back down to the boat. Mothers yelled and grabbed for children as out of the mêlée a beast flew. Hands to our mouths, hoods flung back, we started to run ourselves. Not back to the boat, but on to the beach.

Turning sharply to avoid being caught, the tup had flung itself off the slip, taking something with it: a flash of red hair and yellow coat disappearing in the waves and rain under a solid mass of wool and meat.

The tide was moving swiftly, carrying boy and beast along. Finally they separated. The animal the better swimmer, it recovered more quickly from the shock of the fall.

The skipper was first in the water, a life buoy thrown in after. He grabbed the child in a few desperate strokes and began the eternity to shore, others wading out to meet him.

The boat could not be moved, for fear of those in the water, so the beast could not be saved. We watched the animal struggle, slowly losing its way among the waves, head always up proud, until his calls were dulled by rain and salt and wind.

Over the heads of the boy and his mother we watched. Gathered in her husband's arms she clung to her child, already scrambling for release, as tightly as if she could take him back in to her.

Children have not learned such fear, but we women stood in a line along the spit of land in front of the slip, shoulder to shoulder, as though we could protect our men and our children from whatever lay out beyond the edge of the islands, from the deepness of the sea, with only what was in ourselves. And we watched.

Cold to the bone, your father came to get me, taking my hand and leading me up the beach to the car, to you girls, to our tup, all safely stowed away.

I bought some oilskins, I sent you to swimming lessons. I tried to teach you how to respect the sea. Quaint? Not this island.

Deliverance
by Alison Dawson

Was there ever a night so dark and so terrifying? At first when the engine petered out it was the silence that was scary. The fitful puttering of the outboard had at least meant that they were making some sort of progress, but now the wind had risen and the darkness was filled with the sound of waves splashing against the sides of the boat and that was more frightening than the silence. Were they drifting in the right direction? There was no way of knowing. Amina tightened her hold on Hakim, hoping her closeness would reassure him.

It had all seemed such a good idea so many months ago. Almost an adventure. Their Syrian town had been a thriving conurbation with good schools and lively souks and cafés. Her marriage to an up and coming surgeon had taken her across town, but she was still close to her immediate family and able to continue with her teaching job. She had met Khalid when they were both at university and the arrival of Hakim a year after their marriage had cemented their relationship. The civil war and the emergence of ISIS had changed everything. When the hospital in Damascus was bombed they knew any hope of a viable future in Syria was disappearing and they began to plan.

They decided that Khalid would go ahead to Europe where he could get a job and establish a base prior to Amina and 4-year-old Hakim joining him. Their chosen route through Aleppo then north and into Turkey seemed feasible. Khalid left her with enough money to finance her journey, but they were both ignorant of the fact that he had also left her pregnant.

Travel was difficult, expensive and fraught with threats and delays. It was many weeks since her tearful farewells to her mother and sisters. Syria was now controlled by malevolent and violent madmen. The other areas they had passed through seemed no better and nothing was straightforward. At first she had been able to speak to Khalid on the mobile he had given her, but that had been stolen at the last but one transit camp.

She had told him about the baby and he would be frantic with worry knowing her due date was near.

At the mercy of traffickers, they ended up on the Turkish coast waiting for a space on one of the ramshackle boats plying their unscrupulous trade across the Aegean. By now Amina knew to expect no quarter from these people but there was no way of turning back. It was known among the travellers that the boat would be given enough fuel to get them out into international waters, but not enough to reach the Greek coast. For the latter part of the journey they would be at the mercy of the currents, the tide, and now the wind. Amina and Hakim, having only ever seen pictures of the ocean, were overwhelmed by the endless expanse of constantly moving water on which they drifted. Neither could swim. Life jackets had been offered at an extra cost and Amina had bargained with her last few coins to get one for Hakim. She would manage without. For a split second as she was handed into the boat she met the eyes of the boatman and wondered in panic if he had noticed her stomach as she turned, but he said nothing. Her burka continued to conceal her shape and no doubt saved her a demand for another fare if he had realised he had an undeclared passenger.

The night seemed endless. Amina realised that the absence of stars must mean that the sky had clouded over, increasing the risk of rough weather. About the same time she also realised that her waters had broken. There was so much seawater swilling about in the well of the boat that her plight would be undetectable but nevertheless her heart filled with dread. She couldn't think of a worse predicament than going into labour now. As things would have it, she was the only woman on this boat. Her fellow travellers were men and a mix of nationalities. Definitely not midwife material. And what could she do about Hakim? If they could just reach land she might be able to find help. Hakim knew she was going to give him a little brother or sister; holding him close, she tried to explain what was going to happen without alarming him too much. He seemed to understand but said nothing.　But then he hadn't spoken for months now.　Previously a bright, active little boy who never stopped asking questions, he had been so traumatised by the horrors of this hellish journey that he had become totally silent.　Always fearful now, he never left her side.　It was weeks since they had eaten properly and she knew he was thirsty.　A young African beside them had let Hakim drink from his bottle, but that was finished now.

Hours dragged by until - was it her imagination or was the sky lightening in the east?　Trying to ignore the spasmodic contractions in her abdomen, Amina was startled by some of the passengers shouting and pointing.　Turning to look, she could see in the strengthening light the outline of land on the horizon.　Would they make it in time? Some of the men began trying to paddle with whatever they could find to improvise as oars - mainly their hands.　Would they make landfall before her baby was born? Amina's contractions were now stronger and closer together.　She knew this baby was coming soon and the pain was agonising.

As they neared shore the boat encountered rocks and surf. With no means of steering it was soon in difficulty. Some of the men began to stand up, shouting and waving at distant figures on the approaching beach. It was terrifying. Amina tried to keep hold of Hakim as the wildly rocking boat suddenly capsized, throwing everyone into the water. She gasped as she fell, knowing that she had lost her hold on Hakim. Doubled up in pain she sank, unaware that the surf was carrying her towards the shore. Struggling to the surface again, she shouted for Hakim before the next wave swept over her. Then nothing seemed to matter anymore. Hakim was gone and the pain of labour was all consuming. She couldn't fight any longer and accepted that her life was going to end here.

All along the beach men were stumbling out of the surf and collapsing. Help was coming as men and women from various aid agencies ran to assist the survivors. The bodies of the drowned floated off shore, to be recovered later.

The tall American doctor working on a spluttering black youth could no longer ignore the child tugging at his shirt. "This one will live. Over to you." he shouted to a nearby colleague, "now, what do you want, son?" The boy pulled him towards what seemed like a crumpled heap of clothes deposited at the sea's edge. A woman in a burka. He turned the body over, ready to ascertain death, but paused. There was a pulse, then a groan followed by a convulsion of the body. He checked further then yelled urgently. "Quick! We need a stretcher here. She's alive, but only just and I think she's in labour!"

Amina knew little of the next few hours as her battered body struggled to live and deliver itself of the infant. The sun was sinking when she came to in the cool tent as the doctor and nurse came to check on her. Beside her cot there was a cardboard box and the doctor bent down to lift the small bundle it held.

"I'm afraid we're not really geared for maternity cases here so we had to find an alternative cradle for your daughter. Are you ready to meet her now?"

He gently placed the baby in her improvised shawl in Amina's outstretched arms.

"She's small but she sure is a tough one. I think she'll be fine now."

Speechless with wonderment and relief, Amina looked around - and there he was at the end of the bed.

"Hakim - you're alive! I thought I had lost you." Then he was by her side, gazing at his new sister with his mother's arm around him.

"That's a very brave boy you've got there", said the doctor. "He saved your life by pestering me to come and check on you when we thought you were just another corpse. You can be proud of him."

"I always am", said Amina, surprising the doctor with her command of English.

"You both need to rest now", said the nurse. "I'll bring you some food later. Your little boy has already been fed."

As they left the tent the nurse turned to the doctor.

"Do you want me to take the child to the children's tent? He could be cared for there."

"No, leave him with her. They've been through a lot together and I wouldn't want to separate them, especially since he doesn't seem able to speak," said the medic.

"That seems odd at his age," replied the nurse. "Do you think he is dumb?"

"More likely traumatised. I've seen it before. These children have experienced and witnessed things no child should ever have to and some become elective mutes. His only hope is to stay with his mother and maybe in time he will talk again."

Later, in the quiet dusk of the evening, Amina looked at her son curled into her side in the cot, sleeping the sleep of the exhausted. When she turned to her daughter the baby was awake and she smiled at the solemn, unfocussed stare.

"Welcome to the world, my daughter. Your name is Amal. It means 'hope' in the language of the new country which will be our home. Inshallah - God willing."

Eternal Rest
by Sylvia Smith

The huge black hull sliced through the water, breaking white foam out of the green, curling waves. It headed towards the land, neither slowing nor stopping. It mounted the quayside, crashing through the bollards and barriers. Transfixed, he stared up as it towered above him, ready to drop, to crush him. Ali shouted himself awake. The nausea, the sweat and the terror was real enough. It was always the same nightmare.

Ali swung his feet out of the hard, narrow bed and padded barefoot to the window. To the east, the orange glow of city lights pushed up into the blackness. He dressed quietly. He surveyed the sparse furnishings, his eyes finally resting on the package that sat on the floor beside his backpack. This was his last mission, one he could not avoid. He crossed the hallway. He stepped out into the February morning. Opening the front passenger door of the frosted car, he carefully wedged the package in the foot well. The brown paper wrapping felt shiny and the white string, tight, but not too tight, gave it an old-fashioned look. Tenderly, he tucked his black jacket round it as though it were a baby in a cradle.

He drove cautiously along the icy country road until it joined the motorway. Ali had allowed himself six hours to reach the ferry terminal. He drove north, oblivious to the splendid scenery until he saw the rainbow curve of the Skye Bridge. He was pleased with his progress. As he crossed the island he found himself frequently stuck behind batches of sluggish traffic. His carefully planned schedule was slipping away from him. He began to panic. After a couple of crazy pieces of overtaking he turned the final corner; where the dark green headland opposite towered over the bay, opening out beneath him like a giant bathtub. Alongside the pier, the ferry strained headfirst into the wind, clouds of thick smoke streaming from her funnel. She was ready to sail.

He sped through the village, heedless of the speed limit. In the empty ferry lanes, a man in a high visibility jacket waved a clipboard at him. Ali's heart was beating like a drum.

"Ticket?" The man's voice was snatched away by the wind.

Ali nodded and reached into his pocket.

"Boarding pass?"

Ali shook his head. The man handed him the white card. He scribbled a name.

"Man, you're lucky today! We're waiting for the bus passengers." He pointed to the Citylink bus, rumbling down the hill towards the village.

Ali drove gently along the pier. He crept forward into the cavernous deck, like Jonah going in to the belly of the whale. As the front wheels hit the metal ramp, it jolted against the pier; Ali glanced anxiously at his parcel wedged on the floor. He sighed and wished for the old days, the days before the disaster that was the *Herald of Free Enterprise*, when he could have stayed unobtrusively in his vehicle, on the car deck.

Exiting the car, he shouldered his backpack. Slipping his gloved fingers into the string of the package, he squeezed his way between the other vehicles. The smell of stale, enclosed exhaust fumes filled his lungs, making him cough. He noted the Army vehicles, on their way to military exercises on the island. He had not expected this. He made his way towards the stairway. He zipped up his black weatherproof jacket and pulled his woollen hat down over his ears. Once on the passenger deck he pushed back a heavy door. He stepped out into the fresh air. Engines pulsed under his feet and the salt air stung his nostrils.

Ali watched as the ropes were cast off; he listened to the safety announcements, in English and then in Gaelic. Deep in his memory, seeds of recognition stirred. The propellers churned the grey-green water to white foam. Seagulls followed, hopefully, until the land began to shrink. The nose of the boat rose and fell, sending up plumes of white spray. He licked the salty moisture from his lips. The string from his package began to cut into his fingers. It was time to go inside.

Ali hated the black boats with their white and orange paint. He had stood on a quayside, his small hand tucked in his Grandmother's old work worn hand, and waved goodbye to his mother as she sailed away from them.

"I'll see you soon!" she had whispered in his ear, as she bent to give him a farewell kiss. I'll get a good job, then I'll send for you and granny. We'll be fine!"

But she didn't send for them. A much bigger Ali stood on the same quayside, waiting for her, hoping for the old cosiness and shared whispers, but her eyes were sad, her hair was threaded with grey. Trailing down the gangway behind her were two little girls and a small boy; his half-brother and sisters who stole three quarters of her love and attention, so he hated the boat that brought them. He used to dream about chasing them away, to the man he never knew, who changed his mother's life.

It was many years since Ali had made this journey, and he swore this would be his last. Once he had completed this mission he would never set foot on a ferry again.

Ali went into the cafeteria. Although he was hungry, he felt, at this point, food was a bad idea. Instead he chose black tea. As he sat watching the fluid slop in the cup he tuned in to a conversation at the table behind him. Two elderly ladies, confident that their neighbour did not understand them, chatted loudly in Gaelic, interspersed with modern English words. The old language was coming back to him.

"Do you know that fellow who's sitting behind us?"

"I don't think so. He'll be one of these winter tourists. Photographer or something like that!"

"He's kind of swarthy looking. Do you think he's an American?"

Maybe he's a Mormon! But I thought they always went about in pairs?"

"I hope not. The clergy are supposed to be unlucky on boats. We don't want that."

A ghost of a smile crossed Ali's face.

"You're not so far off the mark, my dear."

The ferry was now out in open water and the horizon appeared and disappeared from the cafeteria window. The early start, the stressful drive and the empty stomach combined; Ali began to feel ill. He made his way to the bar. Perhaps a wee drop of spirits, for medicinal reasons, would sort him out. But he would have to be careful. Drink was another enemy. One drink became two, became three, until he lost count. He stumbled out of the bar towards the blue reclining seats of the television lounge and slept, forgetting all his responsibilities.

The young steward, fresh from his training course, moved around the tables, collecting glasses. He spotted the abandoned backpack and the parcel. Outwardly he did not panic.

He went to the bridge and spoke to the captain. A whole process, ready and waiting, swung into action.

"MV LochAulay calling Stornoway coastguard."

The passengers were sent to their lifeboat stations. The crew held their breath and hoped it was all a huge mistake. Meanwhile, slumped in a corner seat, Ali slept, oblivious to the commotion around him.

Making a final sweep of the passenger areas before evacuating the ship, the steward saw movement in what looked like a heap of clothing. He shook the man relentlessly until he got a response. Through half opened eyes Ali registered the white shirt and the black trousers. He heard the voice telling him to move, to get up, and to leave the ship.

He remembered his possessions. He pushed the young man and tried to reach the bar where the bag and the parcel lay together. The steward lunged at him. The ship lurched. They rolled together on the floor. Fired up with fear and adrenalin, he sat on Ali's legs, pinning him down on the rough carpet.

"So you're the evil bastard who wants to blow us all to kingdom come!"

"What are you talking about? You're mad!"

The steward grabbed Ali's arm as he tried to reach into his jacket pocket.

"You're not throwing any switches if I can help it."

"Here!" grunted Ali, "Take my passport."

The man was momentarily distracted as Ali ripped down his zip, revealing the white clerical collar.

"Read it. I'm Father Alisdair McVarish. My mother died on a pilgrimage to the Holy Land.

She was cremated. She's in the parcel. I'm taking her home to be buried."

They both rose warily as the steward bent back the burgundy cover with the gold writing. He studied the photograph. It was a match.

He read out the address.

"St Kentigern's Missionary House, Barnhill, North Ayrshire, Scotland. Jesus. I'm sorry Father, but these days we just can't afford to take any chances."

Sore, tired and disappointed in himself, Ali shook his head, muttering, "And to think it was my mother's dearest wish. To go quietly. Without any fuss."

A Day's Work

by Leonie Charlton

MV Lord of the Isles shivers her wide wake
out from Oban, paralleled by diving gannets

a whale's jawbone swallows us into port
where the pony-man waits on the pier
pretending not to be, darting about
among the outgoing ferry queue -
in horses they call that displacement
behaviour

finally he makes eye contact
stunning me with blues
his long fingers roll a cigarette
like a perfect flute of kelp
left by the sea

he takes my toolbag, this widower
who thrives on unfiltered cigarettes

black coffee and salty air

the tight twists of his hair
spin out in all directions
his beard shines cannach-white
like the sheeps' wool
that gestures from the fences all over this
island

he takes me in a Landrover – full of Radio1
crackle –
to the fields of grazing Eriskay ponies:
a velvet-muzzled dark-eyed herd
their silvers and grays
decorated with zebra stripes and trout spots

some of the ponies have died
leaving areas of loss

we touch and tame and trim hooves
rasps grow blunt

nippers blister the fold

where thumb opposes fingers

and all day long we hear the birds:

goose and gull

skylark and lapwing

stonechat and oystercatcher

yet there's a poultry-shaped silence

the otter came, took the chickens three a

night until they were all gone

says the pony-man, looking away

meanwhile the peacocks – who rest their

plump breasts high on roof ridges at night –

celebrate in an orgy of wide-spread eyes

their man-feathers rattle like pebbles

the sun drops low

we sit with a last cup of coffee

the pony-man tilts his face to a heron flying

in to roost

crosses his legs, wraps one long foot

around the slender ankle of the other
even then he has leg left spare

that's what comes of eating just an egg a day
or perhaps a crab
I wonder, what does it feel like to have
wind sing through your bones and liver?

Later, in the tilting cafeteria
I eat Barra-landed haddock
with Calmac chips, and plump green peas
and feel how my thighs touch
as I lick salt from my fingertips.

Stranger Amongst Chickens
by Mary Topp

Fresh, fleshy meat protrudes from string bags hung outside on the upper deck. All the verandas are dotted with these gifts of dead chicken presented to returning family members during the precious May holiday. The city dwellers are returning with their mementos of rural origins and home. The ferry is full and I am feeling apprehensive. Maybe I should have planned to avoid travelling at the end of the holiday weekend. No one suggested I travel later in the week when I booked the ticket several days ago and secured one of the last berths on the top deck.

Looking over the rail on the lowest deck I watch the river traffic. I count the boats tied to one another passing us. Each has a long low covered hold at the front. Family washing is slung up between poles. The living quarters is a shack placed at the back, behind which rope ties the boat onto the front of the following boat. I count eleven boats in all pulled along together. Further away, two men work at a long oar to propel a smaller boat. The river is busy.

Now it is too dark to see properly and I join the jostling crowds to make my way up to my berth. Groups of Chinese are sitting on the floor in every corridor, some are playing mah-jong, many are drinking tea and everyone is talking. Finally, I reach a crowded central corridor on the top deck flanked on either side by glass sliding doors. Each leads to a glass walled room with just enough room for eight mattresses placed on the floor. The opposite wall consists of more sliding glass doors opening onto the narrow deck hung with chickens. Most of the rooms are already full with Chinese families settling down for the night. I understand the occasional word of the incessant chatter but this causes confusion rather than allowing me the possibility of communication.

I enter Cabin 8 and smile to myself thinking "*Bù hǎo*, not good, but at least I have my own space. No more jostling today." There is room to lie out full length, not a luxury afforded to those settling in the corridor. I nod at my companions and wriggle into my sheet sleeping bag. My rucksack will be my pillow but first I have to remove my contact lens. Slowly I become aware of a male face staring in at me through the glass from the next room. I am subject to that invasive curiosity again.

"No," I tell myself, "Don't be the judge. I am the stranger here." As the ship lights dim I regain my privacy and relax. I remember sitting on the banks of the Yangtze near Poyang Lake, writing a letter home. A crowd gathered pressing close. One man leaned over my shoulder to point at the squiggle across the page. I realised then that he had expected to understand the script. If there is a lack of understanding of the spoken word in China the written characters are drawn on the palm with the opposite forefinger to help communication. Chinese characters have the same meaning regardless of pronunciation. My scribbled writing was indecipherable and therefore strange. Just now I had appeared to be taking my eyes out. I must seem very weird.

Morning comes too quickly. I wake to the smell of pork dumplings and soy sauce. A family of three have flasks of tea and rice porridge. I am also sharing with a group of four young women. One of them is on her way out to get more hot water.

She turns and asks, "Would you like some tea?"

On her return we exchange names. Zhang speaks good English and as the Yangtze muddies and eddies between slowly receding banks we exchange stories, food and drink. Zhang lives in Shanghai and is returning from a visit home to her family. Many Chinese go home for this holiday and she too has been given a chicken to take back to the city.

I don't venture out of the cabin except to elbow my way to the loo, stepping over prone bodies and pushing past the upright versions. I return after a late afternoon foray to a tense atmosphere in the cabin. I am surrounded by heated argument and turn to Zhang for an explanation. They are discussing a recent announcement noting a delay to our arrival at

Yangzhou and consequent change in the state of the tide when we arrive. This means I will have to disembark midstream to a smaller boat. The smaller ferry will arrive in Yangzhou just after midnight, over two hours late. Zhang knows I plan to leave the boat at Yangzhou where I have a hotel booking. How will I get to the hotel? Onward transport will not be easily available at that time of night.

I have become used to being the subject of animated discussion since arriving in China. It continues until Zhang agrees to write a short note for me in Chinese on the back of her Shanghai business card. It states that I am on my way to the Imperial Palace Hotel and need transport.

"Give this to the first policeman you see" Zhang instructs me. "You know the ones in grey-green uniform with black boots and holsters."

"Oh Yes! I know them," I say. I thank her and put the card away. Chinese police removed the film from my camera after I took photographs of the coast in Xiamen two weeks earlier. I hadn't realised Taiwan was just across the water and therefore the coast there was a sensitive area. This was the 1980s.

Later that evening, we all say goodbye and promise to keep in touch, I step over the swirling waters into the smaller ferry. Arriving at the shore I am alone again in the midst of a crowd which quickly disperses. I see the orange glow of an oil drum brazier further along the dimly lit road. Two shadowy figures are sat beside it. Clutching Zhang's card, I move towards them as one stands up to watch my approach.

I recognise his uniform and call out "*ni hao*," before presenting him with Zhang's card. He reads it and signs for me to wait. He disappears up a side street. I hear a loud hammering and a torrent of quick-fired Chinese. Several minutes later a bald, bandy legged old man shuffles into view wearing a dusty Mao jacket over a grey collarless shirt and loose trousers. He collects his bicycle rickshaw and pushes it towards where I am standing.

I climb into the canvas seat with my rucksack, shout "*xièxie*", thank you, to the policeman and settle back. As we pass through narrow shuttered streets I can see the occasional light up a side alley and hear dogs barking. Late arrivals are heating water or cooking dinner on the street outside their homes.

My driver stops at a level crossing and we watch the railway wagons of a long freight train shunt past interminably. I have no idea whether the hotel will still be open. Brakes and clanking disturb my reverie and I exchange glances with the old man in front of me. The train starts up again and all the wagons now pass by in the other direction. Suddenly we are both laughing. He is lumbered with me. He must get me to the hotel or I will become his responsibility. We don't need a shared language; we quite understand each other's predicament.

We are still chuckling when the train finishes shunting back and forwards and the level crossing is clear. Twenty minutes later we arrive at the gatehouse of the hotel. I want some refreshment for my saviour before he returns home and am sickened by the rudeness of the gate keeper who will not allow the rickshaw into the hotel grounds.

I pay my driver plus a generous tip, spluttering "*xièxie, xièxie*" and become a stranger again.

A Hebridean Tail
by Janine Tannahill

My feet tickled the laced waves. How I felt light and small within this place. A vast indigo fresco of etched medieval, towering clouds, roofed this paradise. The radiant Beach rushed ahead in a crescent curve, catching my breath. Doffing its cap, with a graceful bow, it met the Turquoise Sea. She danced her dance of rhythm and time, her hair full of swirls and veils. They held together clasped in a perfection, flawless and magnificent. The speck of the Ferry caught my eye. With shells in bulging pockets and sand caught snug between my toes, I pushed my new feet into damp socks and rushed for home.

Coffee, creates a tension that grates in me. A clenching anxiety grown from indulgence, age and intolerance. The need for it to be just as it should be, causes me to ingratiate myself and appeal to the great quality of empathy that human beings can, at times, offer. Instructions were followed with polite recognition. Shoulders relaxed, I held a grail.

A liquid of the darkest of brown with a treacle tone edging on a winter dark. The colour of a taste that will connect my mouth, body and mind, to a comfort and contentment. Raised eyebrows and glinting eyes, poured the measured malt whisky. The coffee, anticipating to be cooled and creamed by milk shuddered and shimmered into a whirlpool smile of flavour. I was pleased with my decadence and the simple pleasure of it. I made my way towards the deck for the show.

Ardnamurchan light house blinked and stood sideways, gazing with Rhum, Eigg, Muck and Skye. The cooler wind had cleared the deck of the crowds of travellers. I sat still, willing, in the trance of the waves. The rim of the coffee cup rubbed smooth against my lip. The heat warming my hands and the taste easing my heart. I nudged it slowly with my teeth and blew its steam towards Tiree. It sat still, dark and lined, silhouetted, disguised as a horizon as the sun lingering in a sunset, rested on its back. I felt the coolness of the shells as they rattled with my fingers. This was the West Coast dressed in an evening late summer light. Engine sounds rumbled as discreetly as they should. The ferry crept slow steeped in a ritual, through the deep ancient Hebridean seas. My toes twitch, nagged by the sand rolling in my socks.

Out of the blue! A Leviathan. Old silence in its stealth, poised in its grace of centuries, it slipped, between the silken fabric of wise waves and the determined wind towards the evening star, to face me. A tall Tail of Flukes, pitch black. Long and short curves describing its features smooth and clear. Movement was effortless as it drifted down, hidden forever, cloaked in a blanket of wonder and infinity. Submerged, it continued, within a familiar simplicity that human beings yearn to understand. The world as it was, was quiet, only I existed in a magic of distinction, drowned in moment of euphoria within the loneliness of a lifetime. Something wild and forgotten stirred in me. Awake, alive, breathing, seeing, hearing and feeling. My senses sprung in a tang of bliss as every single cell tingled in rebirth. My lumbered body awash, cleansed by a gift of the real, a gift of substance. I saw everything. A clarity of the expanse, a boundless incomprehensible serenity that dissolves nonsense, dismisses repetitive banality and disgraces precious opinion. I was saved… from drowning.

The rim of the coffee cup ran rough against my lips smearing them with the slime of a plastic trail. The coffee had lost its vigour. It tasted bitter and dank. The alcohol twisting it sour. The empty cup, stained with the dark grains, stumbled on its way against the inside of the bin. As the Ferry drew to the distant twilight streets of Oban town it seemed to hesitate, pause, kneeling to the mighty force of the Whale. I moved slowly to each of the four corners of the deck, my own room, papered with dotted lights paned with warm kitchens and settling fires. The trance of waves gently held me as the sand in my socks excited my toes. I thought of the majesty of the crescent beach, the land and the sea and the love they had for each other. I thought of my girl and her vitality. The shells examined for their shape and grooves, she'd store in a glass jar later to be used for jewellery or simple ornaments. An echo announced the journeys end. Oban harbour welcomed its new travellers with their stories and tales. I thought of how I'd tell the tale of the Whale and its touch. It was in there easing my heart. I knew it was out there, always. I knew it was out there, not only for me but for you too.

The Crossing
by Alison Dawson

Emerging from the car deck she made her way over to the rail, watching the last stragglers hurrying anxiously along the pier to catch the gangway as the crew prepared to close the doors. No sign of the man in black and she began to hope she had been mistaken. The glimpse of the tall figure striding into the booking office as she waited in the car queue had after all been fleeting. The last rope was cast off and the ferry moved slowly out as the captain went into the lilting Gaelic intonation of the safety at sea announcement, preceded by the usual musical 'ping pongs' which brought a smile and a welcome sense of relaxation. The same sequence of notes had been the ringtone of her flat doorbell and she had often been tempted to greet callers with the "Failte à Caledonian MacBrayne" announcement.

The drive from the city had taken a toll on her diminishing reserves of energy and she was glad to find a sheltered seat in the lee of the funnel from where she could watch the broad seascape opening out before her. The steady throb of the diesel engines was reassuring and she drank in the tangy smell of the ebbing tide. Seagulls, those gimlet-eyed opportunists, wheeled and screeched but she was too accustomed to their presence on the ferry to notice. It was good to be going home. As the mainland shrank away behind her, so the stress of her recent life seemed to distance itself and she breathed more deeply. One of the last projects she had done with her senior class had been about Greek mythology. It was an amusing thought to compare this waterway with the river of Lethe. Called the 'river of forgetfulness', the legend had it that you could drink from it in order to forget your earthly life. If that would mean blotting out her immediate past, she thought sardonically, it was a tempting thought.

The boat was busy and passengers milled around her. People thrown together through circumstance rather than choice, existing singly or in groups within their mutually exclusive bubbles. She recognised the usual stereotypes. Men from the Council and the Department of Agriculture with their suits and laptops congregating in the bar. Coffee would be the drink of choice on the outward journey, but she suspected it would be a stronger tipple on the return trip. The hill walkers, usually in pairs, with their camouflage-like clothing and backpacks with their zips and clips. The returning island women, usually identifiable by their uniform hairstyling, were stowing their boxes of messages and greeting friends prior to a gossip in the cafe. Surely there must be some enterprising young thing in Tobermory or Stornoway or wherever with a knack with the scissors and a spell of training in the city who could spot the obvious business opportunity and open a trendy wee salon. Trouble was they left the island and made their lives elsewhere, as she had done herself. She watched a young couple with an infant, wondering if this was perhaps their first holiday as parents. The changing bag slung over Dad's shoulder looked brand new, as did the carrycot. The sleeping baby looked pretty new too. They fussed and fiddled with their paraphernalia. The girl looked exhausted. Perhaps they'd had an early start, or a disturbed night, or both. "Comes with the territory", she felt like saying. But the mum would find that out for herself soon enough.

It was as she turned to catch a last glimpse of the headland that she saw him. The shock hit her like a blow in the stomach and her hands flew to her mouth to stifle the involuntary cry. He stood at the stern with his back to her, hands in his pockets. Although she couldn't see his face there was no mistaking the black jeans and the black leather jacket, the straight black hair ruffled by the breeze as he stared at the frothing wake. Who was he? Why did she keep seeing him? Why was he on the same boat as her? She remembered the first time she had seen him in the car park at the hospital. The session with the consultant and his ominous advice to "put her affairs in order" had shattered her and she had been fighting tears as she fumbled for her car keys. Something had made her look up and there he was a couple of rows across apparently watching her. She had thought nothing of it at the time, but when she saw him in the supermarket the following week she recognised him as the same man. He seemed quite unaware of her so an easily understood coincidence. Then there he was walking on the opposite side of the street as she came down the steps from the lawyer's office, details of her divorce in her hand. Again, she put it down to coincidence, and the fact that with his height and the all-black clothing he tended to stand out in a crowd. Since then there had been other brief glimpses. Always alone when she spotted him, she had told no one, thinking they would tease her about acquiring a stalker, or accuse her of paranoia. But for him to turn up here was inexplicable and terribly unsettling. She could not dismiss his presence on the same ferry as chance. He was no longer on the periphery of her life, he had become part of it.

She turned back and shrank into her seat, pulling her jacket closer as the wind strengthened on the open water. She mustn't let this man affect her so. She had enough other worries to contend with. He had never approached her or threatened her in any real way so why should his presence seem so personal? She had to think ahead. Let's face it, there was no joy in looking back. Jim leaving her out of a clear blue sky had been a body blow and the subsequent divorce had destroyed her self-esteem. The secure, predictable life she had taken for granted had imploded. Finding the lump so soon afterwards had been tough. The treatment involved endless clinics and debilitating hospital stays and she had finally had to resign her teaching job. The divorce settlement had necessitated selling the flat and it had suddenly seemed time to leave the city, go home and regroup. She yearned to return to the crucible of her being. Perhaps there she could find some sort of solace and healing.

Was it her imagination or was the wind rising? She felt nauseous and had begun to shiver either from cold or shock. Not the best sailor, she had taken a seasickness tablet. Perhaps it was incompatible with her other medication. The world had begun to swim round her and a cold sweat trickled down her back. She laid her head back against the seat and closed her eyes.

"Are you all right, dear?" The kindly voice and the hand on her arm forced her to focus again. "You've gone an awful queer colour."

She opened her eyes to find a round face framed by a white perm hovering over her. "Yes, I'm fine really. Just a bit seasick. It seems to be getting rougher. Perhaps I'll go inside."

"I think that would be wise, dear. A nice cup of tea, that's what you need."

The age-spotted hand patted her arm as she got up - and there he was again, behind the concerned face at the other side of the gangway looking straight at her. The flint grey eyes seemed to bore into her, to see into her soul with a remorseless implacability. Twin lasers of icy steel. Shaken to her core she stumbled to the doorway and took refuge in the cafeteria.

The smell of fried food and today's chicken curry special did nothing to help her nausea but at least it was warmer inside. Not in the least hungry, she nevertheless joined the queue to buy the cup of tea which would allow her to commandeer a table until she felt stronger.

Pushing her tray along to the till she was glad to have something to lean on. Her legs felt like wet string.

"Just a cup of tea, please," she said, fishing in her purse for some change.

"Catriona, is it yourself?" The broad island accent came from behind the counter and she raised her eyes.

"Calum. Good Heavens. Hello."

Completely nonplussed, it was hard to react normally to her old classmate.

"You going home for a break? You look as if you need it. You've lost a terrible weight. They must be working you too hard over there"

"*You should have seen me a couple of months ago*", she thought to herself, "*This is the improved version.*"

To Calum she merely remarked that she just needed some of her mother's home cooking. He had never been the sharpest knife in the drawer and his anxious remark, if tactless, had been well meant.

"How is your Mum?" he enquired. " Haven't seen her for ages. I don't suppose she's down at the ferry much."

"She's fine really, just getting older. She's given up the car so she doesn't get around so much. And I think Donnie next door is doing most of the croft work now."

"Aye, it was always too much for her after your dad died."

"How are things with you anyway, Calum?" She was anxious to move the conversation away from her own situation.

"Oh, you know, just living the dream!"

Catriona fought to suppress a hysterical giggle. The phrase seemed more like something Beyoncé might say in a TV interview rather than a response from a man in his forties dispensing chips on a Hebridean ferry.

"Me and Kirsty got a house on this side of the island. Handy for the school and nearer the pier. It's great."

"Good to see you, Calum. Say 'hi' to Kirsty for me. Better go. I think I'm holding up the queue now."

Sitting at a window table she reflected that, for someone like Calum, this job, and his life in general, really was living the dream. It was all he had ever wanted or needed and she had no call to disparage his achievement. The encounter had served to bring her back to earth and she felt calmer.

Nursing her mug, she realised that it was time to think practically. This precipitate homeward flight wouldn't do. Time to re-evaluate her motives. She had her mother to think of. It was months since she had been back and, in a bid to protect her, it had been easy to shield her mother from the grittier details of her illness. Mum had known nothing of the hair loss, the mouth ulcers and the constant vomiting. It was easy to dissemble on the phone. With the recurrence of the cancer and the grim prognosis, she had to face the fact that she was running out of time, and she understood now that the dark stranger was a factor in this. There could be no other reason for his presence. In the natural way of things, a parent should not have to bury a child. She owed it to her mother to prepare her, perhaps make preliminary arrangements and speak to the minister. She must do what she could to spare her. They would discuss it all together. This spirit of acceptance allowed her to feel constructive and in control for the first time in a while.

Realising that the cafeteria had emptied around her Catriona looked out the window. They were nosing in towards the pier. The tannoy requested that all car drivers return to their vehicles and she made her way down the steep stairway, weaving her way through the queued vehicles to the Corsa. As she inched up the ramp onto the pier she noticed the couple with the baby waving at an older couple. From the family resemblance she assumed that they were excited grandparents. Nice to think that the new parents would get a bit of cosseting for a day or two at least.

No sign of the man in black. It didn't matter. She knew now who he was and there was a certain comfort in the inevitability. Death would not be gainsaid.

Still Travelling

by Bob Toynton

Wet, very wet, and then cold. Nothing else at first. A light filled his vision and his mind, but even this was cold blue-white, green-white light.

And then puzzlement. Where was he, was he alive? The dread hit when the word "who" entered his thoughts. He tried to stop thinking, to empty his mind entirely.

He felt as if he were clinging to the sheer smooth cliff of the moment. To loosen his grip would be to fall. Looking down, looking back terrified him. It couldn't be done. To tilt his head would be to unbalance and topple into space. Looking up was out of the question.

He clung to the shapeless now; cold, wet and heavy. Frozen in body and mind. A thought, let alone a question, could be the whisper which triggered the avalanche.

And then a touch. A warm hand on his, and something halted then slowly moved into reverse. What, in his terrified stillness, had been draining from him, ceased and started to grow again. He opened his eyes cautiously.

There was no cliff, no fall. He was flat on his back looking up. It was safe to think.

The ceiling looked familiar but strange. He tried to place the strip-light, the lit sign at the edge of his vision. It was like looking at a newspaper in a foreign language. He could see everything. The layout and the print were just as they should be, but the words made no sense.

"You are so, so lucky" he heard a woman say, and the movement of the hand holding his betrayed the speaker as the source of the life-saving warmth.

"Lucky?" he said in a voice that reflected the trembling of his whole body.

"You've been given a second chance" came the reply in a different voice, but only the outline of the person's head could be seen against the bright light. Then he realised that the trembling wasn't emanating from his body. The floor was vibrating and moving gently but perceptibly. A mechanical noise permeated everything, but he'd only just noticed. It was like that of a large engine in the distance. "I'm on the ferry?" he murmured, meaning it as a question.

"You're on the ferry" a voice confirmed.

"Where?"

"We're about half way across" the woman replied. Her face looked familiar. A comforting face. A face that seemed full of gentle stories. He felt that he had seen her before, many times.

His mind darted back and forth within the dark chambers of his brain. There was a jolt of impact which allowed no further movement in one direction. Then the sting and uncertainty of ricochet. The grasping at something too slippery to hold, even too fragile to dare touch. Nothing had context. Nothing would stay still in his thoughts.

He decided to choose one object. To take one thing at a time and try to fill the void with some sense of who and where he was. He stared at the glowing green sign over the shoulder of the silhouette. The letters spelt out "*Exodos*" "Greek!" he exclaimed.

"Yes Robbie" came the reply.

He closed his eyes. The name was the seed crystal dropped into a liquid aching to be solid. He knew he was Robbie. That was all it took. From this single fact, thoughts, ideas and memories grew like fat glass needles in all directions. Each one racing the others to fill the void. The growth was so rapid he struggled for breath and heard himself gasping. But that was outside. Inside he wrestled, not now with a terrifying uncertainty, but rather with trying to order and to understand all that he suddenly realised he knew.

He visualised the crystals as they grew and grew, some pale as aquamarine, some straw-yellow, others like tourmaline changing from reds to greens as they extended towards the edges of his mind.

There was too much happening at once. There were ideas which started in one filament but only made sense read across other strands of the same colour. He felt his whole life, his whole experience was being rebooted, not in the form it had been, but in ways which allowed him to read from file to file and make sense where there had always been uncertainty.

"Is he relapsing?" he heard the woman say. "Quite the opposite" came the reply.

As he opened his eyes again, he felt so much calmer. Now he could form the questions he needed to ask.

"Was I in the sea?" "Did you find me?" "Which ferry is this?"

"One at a time" said the person standing.

Moving slightly, the silhouette was disrupted and light glanced on features both young and handsome; or beautiful. The hair was light and slightly curled. The features still half hidden in shadow were those of a young man unembarrassed by his femininity or a young woman confident in her strength.

"You were thrashing about, exhausted. You lost consciousness as I reached out to grab you. You would have perished. You were slipping away."

"But where? It doesn't make sense. What am I doing in Greece? I've been here before, but what am I doing here now?"

"You're not in Greece. You're travelling between places."

"But how come I remember everything except this. I understand everything even more than I think I have ever done before. But not this."

"I know everything about you Robbie, but I can't say I understand you" the standing figure responded in a voice which betrayed an unseen smile. This came like a thunderbolt. Robbie was certain they had never met before.

His mind felt tuned and sharp now. Within a moment he could explore throughout the huge and fragile crystal mass, refracting and reflecting memories and ideas. No, he could find nothing anywhere which linked him to his two rescuers.

"Understand me?" he asked almost resentfully. "You saved me. I'm thankful for that."

"Humour us". The woman's voice had a kindness and a warmth which melted away anxieties and made any resistant thoughts seem mean and churlish.

"What is it you want to understand. I'll help if I can. You've been ill. Seriously ill. You were told to put your affairs in order. You only have a few weeks."

"Yes" Robbie responded. "Cancer. It's in my brain. The last scan… I'm riddled with it. Is that why I can't remember coming here?"

"No. You're in a lucid phase now so you would have remembered. Why were you angry when you were told? Why didn't you just let go. You're well beyond the three score and ten. You've had a longer and happier life than most. You know what's growing and pressing in your brain. That's just part of you. Are you angry with yourself?"

"I've no complaints. I've known some good people. I hope I've done no harm and a bit of good. I've tried at least."

"I know. I know."

"I've never been angry with life. It's not always been easy. Christ, some bits have been tough. Some bits hurt. But we'd tire of daylight if there wasn't night, and, bugger it, we'd probably tire of life if there wasn't death. But I'm not exhausted yet!"

"You mentioned Christ"

"Sorry. Didn't mean to offend. I don't …
I've never believed in any of that. I've
thought what I've thought and I've done what
I've done. It's down to me. If you need a book
to tell you what's right and wrong, there's a
problem somewhere. Written words turn into
weapons for bigots. What we feel … that tells
us what's right and wrong."

"And that's enough?" There was
disappointment in the voice.

"For me. Yes"

"So, is it that you're scared of what will
happen in a few weeks' time? That there will
be nothing. Yours seems a pretty bleak view.
One life then nothing."

"The journey, that's what's important.
I'm loving it. Travelling for hours, for days,
for years – but arriving – that just takes a
moment. If all I bothered about was where I
was going and what it would be like when I
arrived, I'd have traded years of fascination

for the promise of one moment. What a waste. Light, dark, life, death, interest, oblivion" Robbie summarised slowly and quietly.

"Strange choice of words. Interest. Oblivion."

"People, places, creatures, history, ideas, … even politics. Look at anything closely enough, you can't help but be interested. When I stop finding that interest, I'll let go. I know this is all a puzzle, a crossword I'll never finish, but I'm not bored yet. To lose interest. That feels like insulting the world, and if you need a creator, insulting him too."

"Or her" the woman interjected.

"I'll stick with nature. We'll never really understand how it all works. How it came about. It's sheer arrogance to think our poor part-evolved brains, let alone mine, could understand. But that doesn't stop it being fascinating. Doesn't stop me trying."

"And now I'm starting to understand" came the reply.

"Oh, it feels so good to get that off my chest at last. But you still haven't answered my questions. Where are we going? How did I get in the water? And who are you?"

"Home. You weren't in the water. And here they call me Varkaris"

As the words were spoken the engine noise changed, there was an unnerving vibration and Robbie felt the ferry start to turn. Varkaris swayed under the light and for a moment he glimpsed the whole face. Involuntarily Robbie's eyes slammed shut. In that instant the whole fragile crystalline mass in his brain disintegrated into a million glassy shards. In the darkness the floor tilted, and he was back on the cliff, terrified.

He was still wet. Very wet, but no longer cold. Gradually the motion lessened then ceased. It felt safe to open his eyes again.

"*Piso kai pali mazi mas*" said the nurse, holding his hand.

"What. I don't…" Robbie responded

"You speak Greek?" she asked. "You've been speaking Greek".

"No."

"*Varkaris*, you say. *Varkaris*. Over and over. I think it's funny. Very funny" He read her name badge. Maria, and a surname he couldn't pronounce.

"In Greek I said "back with us again". They were powerful drugs you were given. Do more harm than good some say. Are you OK?"

"I'm still interested" Robbie said

"In the trial? I hope so. We don't get many volunteers."

"No - in life" Robbie said almost to himself.

"You are so, so lucky. You've been given a second chance" he heard Maria say as she went to get help to change his bedding.

"What was funny? You said something was very funny" Robbie asked Maria as soon as she returned.

"The consultant. The one who came when you were really bad… Mr. Ferryman."

"Ferryman?"

"Yes. Ferryman. This in Greek is *varkaris*. You said his name. He didn't realise, but I did. And he thinks he knows everything. But no-one here knows everything, do they?"

And Maria smiled a smile of such warmth, and almost imperceptibly raised one eyebrow as if they had shared a secret joke.

The Sea Wife
by Elizabeth A Clark

Damn this weather, only just out of harbour and this stinking squall hits – slowing us down, tossing us around like flotsam and just perhaps forcing us back to port. I glance at the old photo again wondering just which one was gran-gran? Sim, last of her brothers' immediate family might just know, and the plus was, I was getting to meet family just discovered through this same photograph. Tired I rest my eyes, settling as much as possible onto the torture seats. The salt tang sinuously invades my nostrils, as I let myself drift.

My clothes stink of salt, sea and fish; they stand upright at night, my ghostly knight.

My fingers and hands sting with the myriad small cuts from gutting knife, fish bones and encrusted with scales. It's hard to bend them to my task – I cry salt tears, soak my hands in water each night praying for no pain on the morrow.

Each day the cold seeps into my bones that little bit deeper, no longer able to use the barrel fires to keep some warmth in me, I freeze. Hunched over a jewelled-scale encrusted table, dead fish eyeing the surroundings in seeming surprise, salt lying in sparkling diamond mounds.

I huff a laugh at my thoughts. Peigi says that to laugh is important, allowing us to chatter and let our fingers work, concentrating; and yet not; on the slashing, bright steel in our hands, the barrels we pack with the fruits of our trade layering filleted fish and salt to the top.

In similar fashion we use 'the English' as only one other person speaks my Isle of Skye Gaelic, Peigi speaks Doric and Dolena lowlands Gaelic, so English it is. The men comment on our 'thick accents', but we understand each other very well – and the men – which is why we lassies always stay together in the loft, streets and lodgings – we are no' daft.

The gas lights pop, hiss and splutter. Iain 'beag' will have to trim the wicks again. Wavering light casting shadows deeper than those from the perpetual dusky glow coming in the skylights. The clouds chasing faint silver shadows across the loft, gradually fading and then deepening as they reach the walls.

Day upon day, blurring, chilling, numbing. Body unwilling repeats the routine, unthinkingly. Flickers of movement all around, a voice raised in song – not one of us, it's Iain, his voice an odd mix of the child he was and the man he is becoming. Calming, filled with longing, haunting. We all tap time with our clogged feet, hands moving in time with his cadences.

Yet my legs feel like the stone tree stumps back home, my feet and hands are bluer than the sea at midsummer; damp clothes adhering to skin, clinging as limpets do to rocks, even though my clothes are soaking up the damp again the flakes still fall like leaves, a coarse flour from the outer layers – salt, scales and dried gut pieces. They drift off still as I walk to work and fall like sleet as I return to my shared room.

The smells and sounds remain the same, an unchanging daily frame of noise in this sprawling town. Hemp rope, the sea, kelp, fish, salt, damp clothes, seagulls, steam engines, castor oil, fire, coal, dampness, mould, stale air and the rancid smell of hastily washed mankind.

Outside we hear the steam engines chuffing away as they lift the baskets of the silver darlings and other fish, overlying are the cries of the rowdy trawlermen and stevedores. The wheels of the 'barrows' ringing on the cobbles, the clogs clicking away as we all move in a synchronous progression of labour in loft, harbour side, trawler hold, and all watched over by Mr Alexander Woolf, Factor and not someone we want any dealings with. He makes each day a nightmare beyond our white, blue-tinged, swollen fingers, clogs frozen to our feet and our permanently damp clothing.

We walk to the loft in darkness and home in darkness, our meagre pennies spent on the makings for soup, vegetable stew and porridge, cooking in the communal kitchen of lodgings that do not bear the name well – at home we would not byre our cattle in such conditions. Sleep comes hard in crowded rooms, filled with sounds of humanity in distressed slumber, the constant rustle of straw mattresses, the recognisable sound of mice and now town rats in walls, roof and under floorboards. Above all, rises the stench of humanity at its poorest and most helpless. All praying that soon, very soon our coppers and siller will be enough to return home, that our living nightmare will be over.

Each night as we shed our outer garments we check seams and collars for insects and sea-lice, aware that the encrusted clothing will stand sentinel over us, like grey guardians so strong is the solution of salt, scales and fish flesh they stand empty, rigid. The newer fish wives uncertain, the children frightened by our rituals and the phenomena of 'invisible' forces in our clothes.

Still, at the break of each dawn, after my porridge I'll shuffle in cold, clog clad feet back to the loft and the next load of fish. Stiff fingers working their magic, my semi-rigid clothing holding me up, and think of home.

The metallic jarring knocked me off my perch, jerking me awake more effectively than my alarm. Landing hard on the undulating floor, my knees protesting their sudden abuse, as I fling out an arm to steady my swaying body – the sudden realisation of modern sounds, ageless smells and my location had my mind reeling. 'Never done that before' I mutter hoisting myself up, smiling in apologetic embarrassment at the Purser looking in my direction, *damn must have heard my yelp of pain*. I absently massage one badly bruised and aching knee, then flex both knees, only semi-satisfied that all was well.

I try to balance, yet I remained swaying and up-downing in ever diminishing semi-violent bobs. Damn I wasn't imagining it, the vessel was almost corkscrewing itself into the harbour side. A screech of static, and the tannoy boomed out –

'The captain and crew apologise for the storm extending the scheduled time and manner of our arrival at Uig. We ask all foot passengers to wait in the terminal building; drivers and their passengers can exit the ferry but must remain in the area directed to. All ports along the western seaboard of Highland Scotland have been closed due to mega-storm Aimee, and **all** travel has been suspended. We are attempting to make emergency arrangements for your accommodation; food and refreshments will be available free of charge until this situation is resolved. Thank you for travelling with Caledonian-MacBrayne.'

Deafening silence, punctuated by scraping sounds as suitcases, bags, buggies and backpacks were heaved off shelving onto backs. Bairns inserted into buggies. Bags clasped in hands or hung on shoulders. Suitcases hefted or, if they had wheels, dragged alongside. Tired feet on the ends of tired legs which were attached to very tired bodies and heads as the ferry disgorged its passengers, vehicles and freight. I had the feeling that great-grandma was present and laughing.

Ferry To A Lost Future
by Jeni Rankin

Polly and Andrew stood at the handrail, the wind stirring their hair as the engines vibrated pulling *The Claymore* deeper into the water away from the hilly landscape of Craignure. The ferry was crowded with other wedding guests who had congregated in the lounge within easy striking distance of the bar. They had both felt they wanted to prolong the occasion a little longer and opted for fresh air and scenery. Side by side at the rail, they looked at each other and smiled and Andrew looped his arm around her shoulder. As they passed Duart Castle, home of the chiefs of the Clan MacLean, Andrew told her the story of the Lady Rock from the 16th Century. Tiring of his wife, Lady Catherine, Lachlan MacLean had abandoned her on the now renowned skerry at low tide with the intention of her being drowned as the waters rose. Luckily, she was rescued by a passing boat and returned to her brother, Archibald Campbell, the Earl of Argyll. Later her other brother, Sir John, killed MacLean in revenge for the treatment of his sister. Polly loved listening to Andrew's tales although this one sounded a bit harsh; she supposed divorce had not been an option.

Polly felt sorry to be leaving Mull as she had enjoyed herself so much. Weddings were always fun and, if she had any reservations, it was the prospect of meeting so many of Andrew's relatives at once. After a while, she had given up trying to sort out the filigree of family relationships and just enjoyed being in a large group of people who knew each other well. Andrew's relatives appeared to be spread far and wide, but a sizeable proportion of them had managed to congregate on Mull for the wedding of his cousin Mary, whose family lived there. Many of them were crowded into relatives' homes, some even sleeping on floors, and she had been glad they opted for peace and privacy in the faded Victorian splendour of the Western Isles Hotel in Tobermory.

Polly had met Andrew in Edinburgh about three years earlier; he lived with his parents in the suburbs whilst she had a tiny flat in the student area. He was a man of simple tastes, hardworking and honest. She had initially liked him for his casual good looks and gentle ways but had fallen in love with his kindness and easy sense of humour. They were both in their early twenties and neither had had a serious relationship before, they just seemed to fit together really well. They had no real ties and, with him, she had explored European countries on a succession of holidays visiting the places she had heard about but never plucked up the courage to go and see. When they wove their dreams of the future, they even talked of throwing in their jobs, getting an old van and touring round Europe footloose and fancy free. Everyone wanted to do something like that in the '60s.

Polly had worked as an agency temp until she found a job she really liked and soon gained the promotion she wanted so much. Plans on travelling to Europe were shelved as she explained she wanted to build a 'proper' career. Andrew had been very disappointed and the VW van he had been doing up stayed in his parents' garage for a long time; then came this wedding.

As they stood at the rail watching the widening sea, they had fallen into companionable silence and, as Polly gazed out, she found herself thinking she would find their parting difficult, her returning to her one room flat and Andrew back with his parents. To cheer herself up, she thought back to the wedding itself, and how she had been able to indulge in being an inveterate people watcher. The church ceremony is always the most exciting part with all its pageantry. It is the more formal dance before the raucous upheaval of the reception with its collection of in-laws, outlaws and those who are not too sure, and the inevitable parade of over inebriated uncles and hairy chinned aunts.

When they entered the Tobermory Church holding hands it was already quite crowded, but they were ushered towards the front pews. The resonant tones of the organ seemed to tremble through their feet on the flags. The smells mingled together: the furniture polish used to bring the dark wood to its bright shine, the slightly musty tang of the old hymn books, the waxy scent of the candles and the waft of flowers. Polly had looked up at the high vaulted ceiling with its dark beams against the cream of the paint. A flash of light had caught her eye and she saw the sun stencilling through the stained glass, lighting the dust motes floating leisurely in the air. There was a hum of conversation as old friendships were renewed and scattered families congregated together.

As Polly looked around she wondered if she was a tad underdressed, she had forsaken her beloved bellbottom jeans for a long floral dress and, as a concession to the occasion, had wound a flower in her hair. Andrew was bedecked in his kilt and full formal dress and she thought he looked very handsome. She took in the arrays of women with their cauliflower perms and lampshade hats squashed on their heads like pressure cooker lids. They stood tight in their crimplene suits, bulky handbags clutched on their arms. The younger girls had long hair worn loose and were exposing daring amounts of thigh in their mini-skirts. The men who had not braved the kilt were pressed awkwardly into suits, fingering the collars of their shirts.

As they chatted to people around them, they heard the first few chords of Wagner's chorus and, with a shuffling of feet, everyone was up. As if as one, they all turned to admire the lovely bride as she came sedately up the aisle on the arm of her enormously proud father and her infectious smile caught them all. The service progressed as services do, prayers were said, hymns were sung and blessings were called for. They could all relax once they had navigated the pregnant pause as the question of anyone knowing 'any just impediments' was explored, and then they could move onto the serious business of exchanging vows and swearing undying love and fidelity to each other. Polly noticed the bride promised to 'obey' her husband which made her raise a metaphorical eyebrow. The service continued to the final prayers and blessings before the first triumphant chords of Mendelssohn's march reverberated around the vaulted ceiling to an accompaniment of some sniffling and nose blowing.

Polly smiled in her reverie and Andrew looked at her.

"What are you smiling about?"

"Oh, just the wedding" she said, "it was such fun."

"I'm glad you enjoyed it, families can be a bit daunting *en masse*, particularly mine!"

She laughed, "It was a bit of a baptism of fire, but I still enjoyed it all, especially the reception." She reached over and covered his hand with hers. As she looked up at him she thought she saw a trace of sadness in his eyes. He paused a moment then said:

"Why did you laugh when they asked when we were going to get married?"

Polly looked up at him puzzled wondering what he meant. She thought about the uproar of the reception with its loud music and press of people. She remembered Andrew whirling her round the dance floor as did a few other laughing, kilted men who were happy to direct her steps if she lost her way. She recalled some of the older generation leering towards her and saying:

"You're next!" Or: "When are you two going to get married?"

Polly thought about why it made her laugh.

"Well, it was so cheeky!"

"But why did you add 'no way'?"

"Well, we don't want to get married, do we? We're quite happy rubbing along as we are."

"Why do you say that?"

Polly looked at him quizzically. "Well we are, aren't we?"

"Well no, I'd like to get married."

She gave a small gasp, "What?" it came out louder than she intended and she put her hand on Andrew's arm to soften her words and wondered where all this was coming from. Perhaps Andrew was being swept away by the romance of the wedding.

He took her hand, "Will you marry me?"

She sighed, "Oh Andrew, we want completely different things for our futures."

"What do you mean?"

"Well, you want a nice domesticated wife who'll give you 2.2 children and have your pipe and slippers warming by the fire every night when you get home." Andrew smiled so Polly ploughed on: "But you know I don't want children and I'm not really properly house trained. Anyway, I've got a good job now and I'd like to get on, maybe go for more promotion."

Andrew looked nonplussed. "Why can't you do that when we're married?"

"But how about children? It's such a big thing Drew, it's not exactly something we can compromise on."

"I was hoping you'd change your mind" he said with a hopeful grin.

"No, I'm sorry Drew, I'm certain I don't want to have children."

"Then we won't have children, I just want to be with you."

Polly looked into his eyes and almost fancied she saw his children crying to be born.

"No," she said, "if either of us made such a big compromise we'd end up making each other totally miserable and we'd be divorced by the time we're thirty, I don't want to get married like that." She realised Andrew was still holding her hand and she gently disengaged from him.

"Let's talk about it later. We've had such a good time at the wedding and I loved meeting all your family."

Andrew looked at her in thoughtful silence. "I think I need a drink" he said finally.

Polly rubbed her hand affectionately down his arm. "Good idea, get me one in and I'll be down in a minute." She watched him until he disappeared through the door.

Turning back to the rail and gazing out as the ferry continued across Loch Linnhe towards Oban, she wondered where they would go from here. The question had been asked and could not be unasked. The answer had been given and would not be forgotten. She wondered how she could keep Andrew in a relationship that wasn't going where he desired. That would not be fair. As she pushed these thoughts around she realised there was another question to be asked. If she felt they could not marry, did she love him enough to let him go? She felt the tears well in her eyes as the question tugged at her heart.

She knew, although they wouldn't talk about it today, they would have to talk about it soon and she knew what she'd have to say. She already realised these issues might be the rock upon which their relationship would founder. As surely as the ferry had left Mull, as much as she loved him, she would have to let Andrew slip his moorings and drift away.

Morag
by Alex Breck

We had escaped to our new life of freedom and at that point everything had seemed possible.

The first ferry of the day had left on time for a refreshing change. The sun was blindingly bright and as the flecks of snow-white spray splashed our upturned excited faces, I remember thinking she was the most beautiful thing I had ever seen.

I'd hidden in the overgrown bracken by old MacPherson's cottage since daybreak, terrified someone would see the steam from my panicked breath, it was that cold. It was impossible to keep still and my mind raced with the implications of what we were about to do. I felt horrible about leaving my family, but deep down I knew they'd be on our side. I loved this girl more than anything and it was time to stop hiding away like we were doing something wrong. It wasn't like we were kids anymore and besides, we'd not done anything like that anyway.

My love for Morag was pure and unsullied and when I held her hand as we walked up the gangway it felt as profound as walking up the aisle. But that had been the main problem. Morag was from the local church, the Free Church of Scotland, *An Eaglais Shaorin* in the Gaelic, whereas my family were from the Catholic side of things although I'd never stepped inside any church since my granddad's death fifteen years back.

We couldn't have cared less about all of that but for some reason these historical distinctions were somehow etched into our family's DNA like some hereditary disease. The two of us would hold hands and stare deeply into each other's eyes and swear our undying love for one another. I had a special name for her. I called her *Morag the toerag*. Yet inside, we both understood that this genetic curse couldn't be altered no matter what we might wish for. And so, despite being best friends for ever, there was no chance we'd ever be allowed to get married.

I hadn't explicitly told a soul that I was leaving that morning but, looking back, the signs would have been there. I had badgered my best pal Angus to buy my record collection off me, even my treasured old punk LPs which he'd hated. My folks had thought I was saving up to buy Jeannie Robertson's old Mini, seeing as she had gone to the college over in Inverness but when I'd thrown all my tapes into the bargain, the shocked look in Angus's eyes told me he'd guessed what I was planning. I saw avarice and mischief battle for dominance as I handed him my Swiss Army Knife, my Newton's Cradle and then my hidden stash of unused Durex, surreptitiously bought on the school trip to see Macbeth last autumn.

Donald the ferryman hadn't been his usual loquacious self that morning. Normally the conduit of the best (and worst) gossip for the entire community, he had been tight-lipped and gruff when I'd handed over the cash for our tickets. He remained ensconced in his metal box which was the purser's office, which he never normally did and he slid the tickets across the counter with a look that said, 'do you really want to do this?' The sweat-damp tenner had probably given me away and I realise now that it hadn't been anger or even disapproval I'd seen in his face. It had been fear.

But we were filled with youthful optimism and we hardly noticed the bracing breeze from the north. It would have been just one of many portents of things to come that I should have seen. As the early morning sun became warmer we leant over the side of the ship and marvelled at the shapes in the water. The light seemed to reflect off the waves and sparkle in Morag's huge blue-green eyes and we held each other tight. I can't remember which one of us suggested it first but something in those eyes, with her freckled button-nose pressed hard to mine, made my head spin and within moments we were lost. It didn't take us long to tear the clothes off each other and against the rusting bulwark of the cramped toilets, we made love for the first time. Laughably awkward and hopelessly unromantic, we nevertheless sealed our love and with it, our fate.

I will think back to the rest of that ferry journey every day of my life for it was unquestionably the very best day of my life. Sunshine had never looked as beautiful as when it lit up Morag's eyes and her red cheeks glowed with a fire no sun could ever match. The deep green of the flat calm sea contrasted with the untamed curls of her fiery red hair and we laughed until our bodies ached. We laughed at the gulls trying to steal a crisp from my outstretched hand and even the shapes in the clouds had us giggling like schoolgirls. I remember our legs had felt shaky like never before after the intensity of our passionate activity and we had clung to each other like drunken sailors as we staggered down to the cafeteria. Even the standard-issue cheese toasties and stewed tea had seemed like a banquet to the pair of us that morning.

The plan had been to crash with a second-cousin of mine who had a student flat in Glasgow and from there we'd find jobs and get a place of our own. To begin with, the money in our pockets had seemed like a fortune and I had a kitchen job in a trendy bar-restaurant within a few days. We gorged ourselves on new experiences like take-away food and pubs that stayed open all day, even on a Sunday. We splurged our dwindling reserves on taxis' and clothes and before we knew it, we were skint.

Morag became moody and wouldn't go drinking with me, not even for free when I was promoted from the kitchen to serving behind the bar. She said she missed her mother and suggested we go back to the island and come clean about what we wanted to do. We both knew it would be dangerous and when I found out she'd already phoned home, I flew into a rage. But I still thought we were invincible and so agreed to get the afternoon ferry the following Monday, after I had done a lunchtime shift at the pub. Morag said she'd meet me at the ferry terminal and that morning was the last time I ever saw her.

Three guys jumped me as I left the pub and I couldn't stop them putting a bag over my head and throwing me into the back of a van. The next thing I knew was when my universe exploded into a kaleidoscope of light and when I awoke, I found myself tied to a chair in some dingy basement. Morag's father Hughie was there, with one of her brothers.

"You'll be needing some money to keep you going in this city of sin, will ye not?" Hughie said.

He was trying to be reasonable, I can see that with the benefit of hindsight, but at the time, I didn't realise how much trouble I was in. I spat in his face. A massive fist hit me so hard in my stomach that I fell backwards and knocked myself out on the floor. I came to as they man-handled me back up whereupon Hughie punched my face again and again until I saw one of my own teeth embedded in his meaty knuckle.

Unable to speak, I simply nodded like an imbecile as Hughie spelt out what was going to happen. I was never to see Morag. I was forbidden to contact her and if I ever got on that ferry again, he would kill me.

So, they left me there. Just to make sure I'd got the point, Morag's brother broke my leg with a length of wood and now almost a year later, I'm still walking with a limp. I took the money left lying beside me on that basement floor. I live in Newcastle now where I got a job at the docks. I've heard she got married to my old pal Angus and they've had a wee girl already. They say she's just as bonnie as her mother, as if there could ever be another. Every day I look at the ships coming and going and I think of that ferry, resplendent in its coat of red and white paint and standing there alone on the deck with the sunshine and the waves, I see Morag.